This book belongs to

____

to Mahki
"We love you!"

"TO ALL THE CURIOUS
LITTLE PEOPLE OUT THERE,
THIS IS FOR YOU! "

~Ashley B.

DEAR READER.

This is a very funny & engaging book.
WHEN YOU READ "SNIFF. SNIFF."
BREATHE THROUGH YOUR NOSE
&
Point to the listener(s)
To say......

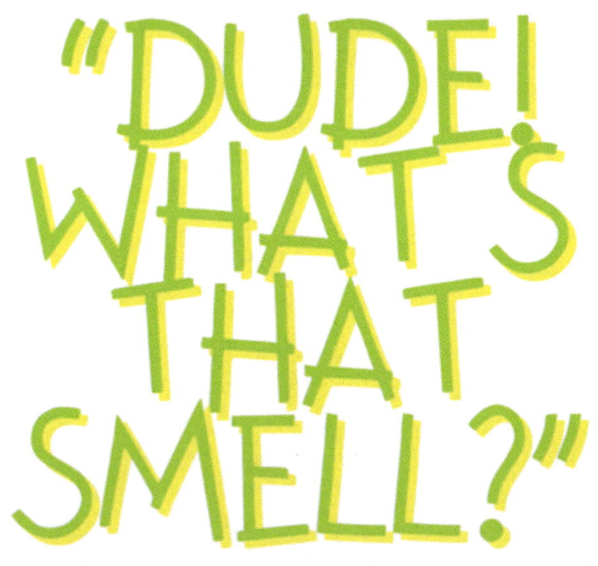

1

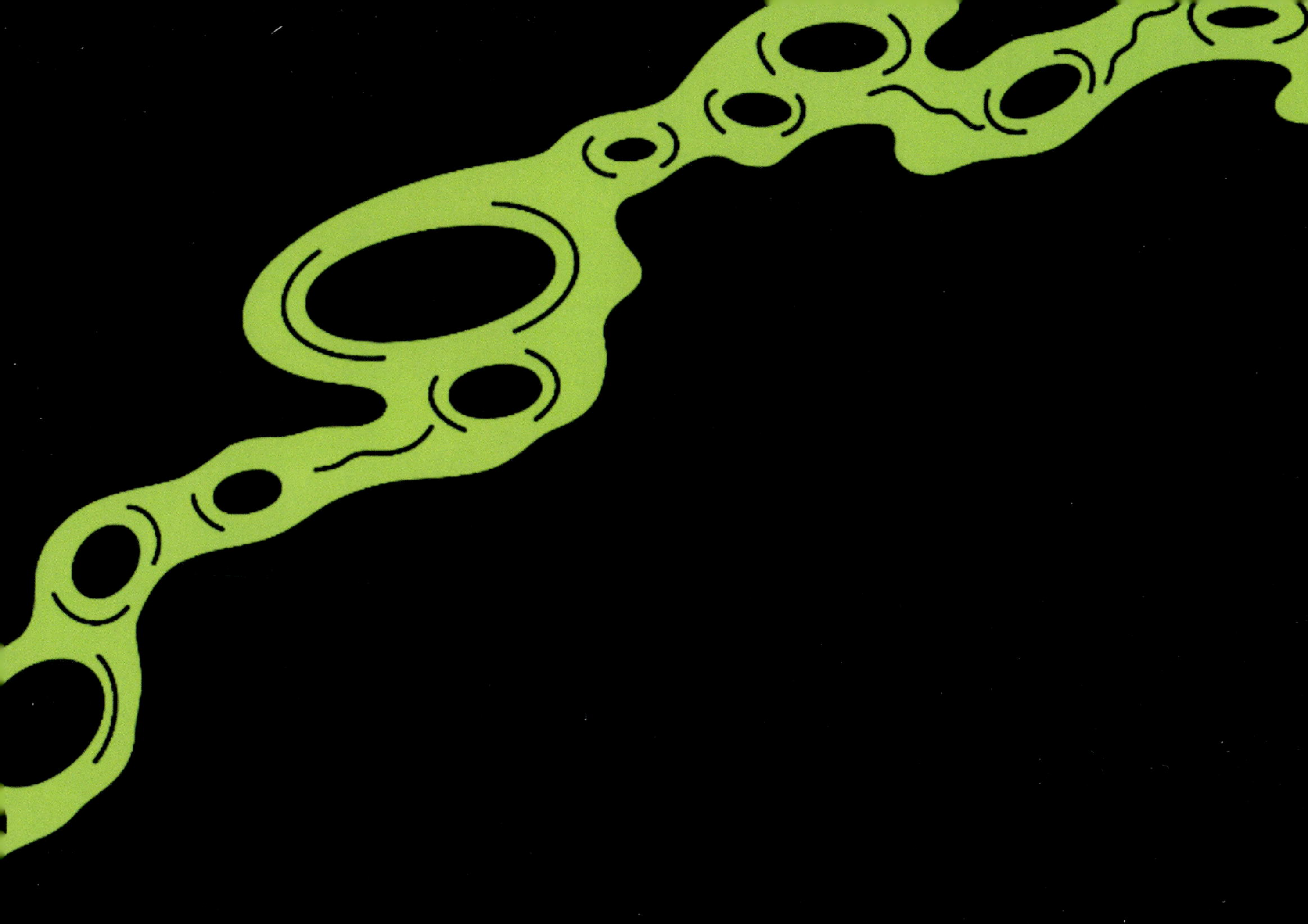

Sniff.

Dude!

WHAT'S THAT SMELL?

Z was awakened to a mysterious ODOR.
Invaded from his dreams,
the STENCH was a torture.
So awful he couldn't even
recognize and tell.
Sniff. Sniff.
"DUDE! WHAT'S THAT SMELL?"

4

5

There was no way on earth, Z could fall back to sleep.
Desperately, searching around his room, and came in contact with A.J's his big brother's FUNKY feet!
It was a fact his brother's feet REEKED!
After all, he played quarterback on his high-school's football team.
But, to no avail.
That was not the smell.
Z, had only one question...
Sniff. Sniff.
"DUDE! WHAT'S THAT SMELL?"

7

Z made a dash to the
bathroom sink.
He let out a huff, and sure
morning breath STINK!
But, to no avail. That was
not the smell.
Z, had only one question....
Sniff. Sniff.
"DUDE! WHAT'S THAT SMELL?"

AJ-16yr's
Z-5yr's
4yr's
Ohh
9

Now the mission was on,
as the WHIFF became strong.
Z followed his nose, to his dad
without clothes!
What a awkward moment, as dad
strained on the toilet!
But, to no avail.
That was not the smell.
Z, had only one question....

Sniff. Sniff.
"DUDE! WHAT'S THAT SMELL?"

11

Safe and sound.

Z found his way into his parents room.

Into a cloud and AROMA, of BURNING ceramic hair irons and POLLUTED perfume!

Mom to busy getting pretty for a lunch date out with dad.

Not even noticing Z, or her favorite FRAGRANCE the family cat had.

But, to no avail.

That was not the smell.

Z, had only one question.....

Sniff. Sniff.

"DUDE! WHAT'S THAT SMELL?"

OOMPH
14

Z was alerted to a loud &
explosive sound. He raced down
the staircase, to his papa
shooting off bombs from his
round! What a horrid sight, as
the VAPORS blasted from under
the blanket! Z held onto dear
life! Afraid, his stomach couldn't
take it!
But, to no avail.
That was not the smell.
Z, had only one question.....
Sniff. Sniff.
"DUDE! WHAT'S THAT SMELL?"

15

PEACE

Z heard the smoke detector, and thought it was the end of the mission. To his surprised, it was his little sister BURNING cookies in the kitchen!

Z low key upset, that the cookies were BURNT!

He had been investigating a smell, that had his belly turnt!

But, to no avail. That was not the smell.

Z, had only one question.....

Sniff. Sniff.

"DUDE! WHAT'S THAT SMELL?"

17

0:00
450°
H
C
18

Z, had searched the house from high to low.

To a basket of MUSTY clothes on the basement floor.

Was this a dirty little joke that his family planned?

Searching for candid cameras, Z thinking to himself,

"THiS not even funny man."

But, to no avail, that was not the smell.

Z, had only one question.....

Sniff. Sniff.

"DUDE! WHAT'S THAT SMELL?"

GRAMP'S
CLOTHE'S
PIC'S
O'S
CD DISC'S
OM & DAD ROOM
ACID
Toxic
20

DUDE WHATS
THAT SMELL?
Sniff. Sniff.
what could it
be?

21

Z, thought he was losing his mind. Thinking to himself, "IS it me?" He thought he had checked everywhere. Everywhere the STENCH could be.

ZEEKIPRO
23

Suspicious of the family's cat.
Z raised the cat by his tail, to find
only his baby brother's toy fishy.

That's it!
Z had checked everywhere.
Everywhere, but baby Ki's room.
Z excitedly raced up the stairs.
In a flash! In a zoom!

Z slowly opened the door,
to baby
Ki'Ki's nursery room.

Dude! OMG! WHAT'S THAT?
It's you!
Captive by the smell.
Being, bum rushed by the
FUMES!
Baby Ki hummed,
" baby shark doo, doo, doo."
Waiting to be discovered
in a SOIL diaper of BOO
BOO!

WEE HEE HEE
26

HA
HA
HA
OM
HHH
HH
27

Baby ki Smirked, as he caught eye
contact with Z.
Sitting in a Stew of poo.
Z Screamed and panic!
Not Sure what to do.

Aj & Papa we're Sleep & out for
the count.
Mom & DAd we're to busy
getting ready to go out.
Baby SiS and the cat, we're Sure
to be no help at all.
'Z, figured It was up to him, to
answer the call.

Baby wipes check. Soap check.
A diaper and clean booties.
Z cleaned up his baby brother.
Hoping not to catch a case of baby
cooties.
Z had wondered how could a baby
smell so awfully bad?
Z knew if he ever smelled this
HORRENDOUS smell again, to first go
grab Mom & Dad.

DEFGHITKLMNOPQRSTUW
31

Baby ki was now, so fresh
and so clean, clean.
Gently falling asleep, in the
loving
arms of his big brother Z.
"What a SMELLY, messy
mission.
Z had thought to himself.
He was sure to receive a
trophy for
"BEST BROTHER OF THE YEAR."
To place, and show off on a
shelf.

Now, to you!
For helping me search and smell.
If you ever catch a scent,
that's very hard to tell.
Just breathe through your nose,
and strongly INHALE.....
Sniff. Sniff.
and say..........

33

DUDE!
WHAT'S THAT SMELL?

The End.

34

Dude! What's That Smell? Vocabulary

Aroma	Odor
Boo Boo	Polluted
Burning	Reeked
Burnt	Smelly
Fragrance	Soil
Fumes	Stench
Funky	Stink
Horrendous	Vapors
Musty	Whiff

Dude! Who's the Author?

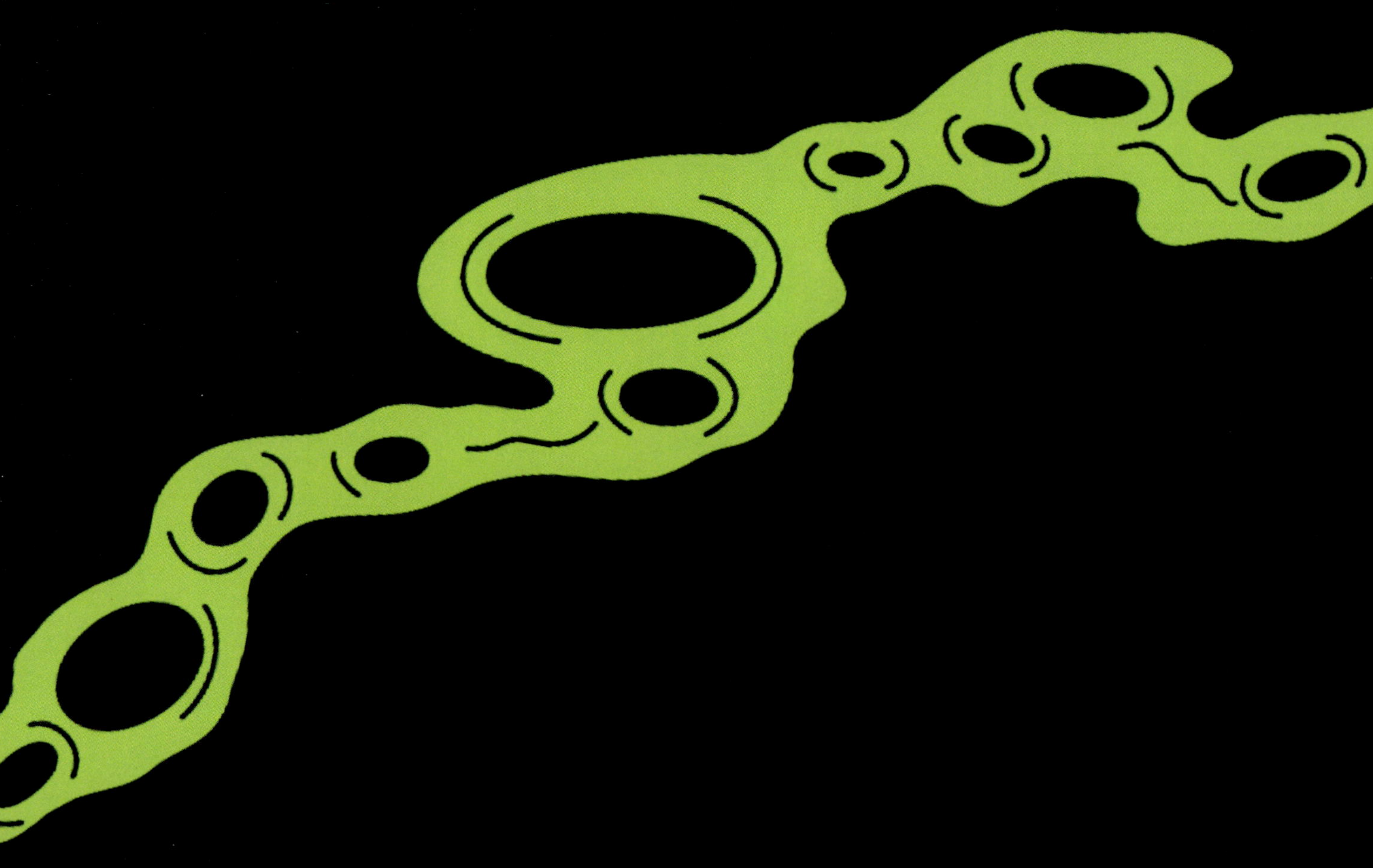

MEET THE AUTHOR

Ashley B.

CREATIVE STORYTELLER & YOUTH ADVOCATE

THE SPIRITUAL GODMOTHER IN THE HOOD, GUIDING THE YOUTH AND COMMUNITY TO FOLLOW THEIR DREAMS & PASSIONS TO CREATE THEIR QUALITY LIVING OF LIFE. SHARING HER MAGIC IN CLEVELAND, OH. TO INSPIRE THOSE SHE MEET TO IDENTIFY THEIR SUPERPOWERS! ASHLEY B. IS THE FOUNDER OF NON~PROFIT ASHLEY B. CHILDHOOD ADVOCATE GUIDING THE YOUTH TO IDENTIFY SELF. FOLLOW AND LEARN MORE ABOUT HOW YOU CAN SUPPORT HER DREAMS AND ORGANIZATION.
XOXO,

ASHLEY B. "PLEASE DON'T FORGET THE B!"

Ashleybchildhoodadvocate@gmail.com
ashleyb_childhoodadvocate

"YOUTH IS TRUTH." -ASHLEY B.

Dude! Who's the Illustrator?

MEET THE ILLUSTRATOR

ZeekiPro

Digital Artist & Designer

My name is Zania J also known as the Artist Zeekipro. I am a young entrepreneur, & Artist from Cleveland, OH. I create ART based off my imagination, creative thinking, surroundings and feeling's.

I speak through my Art so when I create it and share it to the world I hope to inspire others to be true to themselves, to love themselves, to inspire others and the youth, to be kind and to always be Authentic!

Zeekiproductions@gmail.com

Xoxo~ ZeekiPro

Made in the USA
Columbia, SC
10 February 2023

11881492R00024